Healthy Me!

I GET MY REST!

By Kathleen Connors

Gareth Stevens
PUBLISHING

Please visit our website, www.garethstevens.com. For a free color catalog of all our high-quality books, call toll free 1-800-542-2595 or fax 1-877-542-2596.

Library of Congress Cataloging-in-Publication Data
Names: Connors, Kathleen, author.
Title: I get my rest! / Kathleen Connors.
Description: New York : Gareth Stevens Publishing, [2023] | Series: Healthy me! | Includes index.
Identifiers: LCCN 2021037106 (print) | LCCN 2021037107 (ebook) | ISBN 9781538275405 (set) | ISBN 9781538275412 (library binding) | ISBN 9781538275399 (paperback) | ISBN 9781538275429 (ebook)
Subjects: LCSH: Children–Sleep–Juvenile literature. | Rest–Juvenile literature.
Classification: LCC BF723.S45 C66 2023 (print) | LCC BF723.S45 (ebook) | DDC 154.6083–dc23
LC record available at https://lccn.loc.gov/2021037106
LC ebook record available at https://lccn.loc.gov/2021037107

First Edition

Published in 2023 by
Gareth Stevens Publishing
29 East 21st Street
New York, NY 10010

Copyright © 2023 Gareth Stevens Publishing

Editor: Kristen Nelson
Designer: Michael Flynn

Photo credits: Cover StockImageFactory.com/Shutterstock.com; p. 1 LeManna/Shutterstock.com; pp. 5, 24 Rido/Shutterstock.com; p. 7 Ruslan Huzau/Shutterstock.com; pp. 9, 24 Africa Studio/Shutterstock.com; pp. 11, 13, 24 thaisign/Shutterstock.com; p. 15 Gorynvd/Shutterstock.com; p. 17 Yuganov Konstantin/Shutterstock.com; pp. 19, 21, 23 elena_prosvirova/Shutterstock.com;

All rights reserved. No part of this book may be reproduced in any form without permission in writing from the publisher, except by a reviewer.

Printed in the United States of America

Some of the images in this book illustrate individuals who are models. The depictions do not imply actual situations or events.

CPSIA compliance information: Batch #CSGS23: For further information contact Gareth Stevens, New York, New York at 1-800-542-2595.

Find us on

Contents

We all need rest.
We grow when we rest!

Naps are short periods of rest. They are during the day.

Bethany takes a nap after lunch. She is tired from playing!

Zach goes to the beach.
It is hot out.

Zach needs a break.
He sits in the shade.
This is rest too!

Terry plays a
soccer game.
He runs a lot.
Time to rest!

We all need to sleep at night.
This is when our bodies grow and repair.

Mom says it is bedtime.
Chase does not
feel tired.
He wants to play!

He takes a bath.
This helps him
feel sleepy.

Mom turns out the light.
Time for bed!

Words to Know

bedtime

break

nap

Index